Walt Disney's
Old Yeller

This edition published by
W H Smith Publishers, Canada.
Produced by
Twin Books
15 Sherwood Place
Greenwich, CT. 06830
© 1990 The Walt Disney Company
All rights reserved.
ISBN 0-88665-883-7
Image adaptation by Van Gool-Lefevre-Loiseaux
Printed in Hong Kong

Walt Disney's
Old Yeller

Twin Books   B. Mitchell

This is the story of Old Yeller—hunter, cow dog, companion and protector. In frontier days, they called him "the best doggone dog in the West." But he sure got into a lot of trouble, too! His story begins one hot summer day a long time ago down in Texas...

Katie Coates stood at the cabin door and watched her son Arliss try to scramble up onto his father's horse. Smiling, his father reached down and swung Arliss up onto his saddle.

"Will you really be gone three months, Papa?" asked the
small boy. "I want to go on the cattle drive with you!"

"It's too long a ride from Texas to Kansas, son," replied
Jim Coates. "Stay here and help your mama and your
brother Travis around the ranch."

"Oh, all right," said Arliss. Then he jumped down and
went looking for his big brother.

Meanwhile, Travis was plowing beside the cornfield. Suddenly, a big yellow dog chased a rabbit out of the corn. Jumper, the mule, was so startled he bolted and ran away with the plow. "Whoa!" yelled Travis. But Jumper broke right through the fence and kept on going.

Travis threw a rock at the dog. "Get out, you crazy, fool dog!" he shouted angrily. The dog ran off, and Travis chased Jumper through the broken fence. It was a long time before Jumper calmed down enough to stop running.

A week later, Travis came home after a hard day's work and found Arliss hugging a stray dog. "Mama!" stormed Travis. "That's the dog that stampeded Jumper and wrecked the fence!" He picked up a stick to chase the dog away.

"Don't you dare hit my dog!" cried Arliss.

"Oh, let him be, Travis," said Katie. "Looks like we've got ourselves a dog."

"Ugly old yeller stray," muttered Travis in disgust.

The next day, when Arliss was
exploring the edge of the woods near
the cabin, he found a bear cub hunting
berries.

"Here, boy!" called Arliss playfully.
When the cub started to run away from
him, Arliss grabbed the cub's paw. He
didn't see the angry mother bear
approaching.

Katie, looking downhill from the cabin, saw the mother bear about to attack her son.

"Arliss!" screamed Katie from the yard. "Turn the cub loose!"

Travis saw the danger, too. "Watch out!" he yelled.

Arliss, hearing them yell and turning around, saw the bear for the first time.

The bear was only a few feet away from the boy when Old Yeller raced out of the yard. Barking wildly, the dog backed the bear around in a circle, allowing Arliss to escape to the cabin.

When Old Yeller returned to the cabin later, he was welcomed as a hero. "You crazy, fool dog," said Travis admiringly. "You could have got yourself killed!"

"Good dog!" said Katie warmly.

"Told you so," said Arliss.

"Well, he's a heap more dog than I had him figured for," admitted Travis.

One hot day, Bud Searcy and his daughter Lisbeth dropped in to visit. "Lot of thievin' in the neighborhood, Mrs. Coates," said Searcy. "Meat stolen out of smokehouses, hens' nests robbed. Folks say it's probably the work of that dog that strayed off Burn Sanderson's place last week. He looks a lot like that yeller dog of yours I saw out front."

"Well, he's *not!*" said Arliss, slipping his arm around his mother. A secret look passed between Katie and Travis. They were both relieved to say good-bye to Bud and Lisbeth when they finally left.

A few days later, Rose, the family cow, didn't return from the pasture for the night. "I figure she's hid out somewhere and had her calf," said Katie to Travis. "Be careful when you find her. She'll be in a fighting mood."

During the hunt for Rose, Old Yeller proved to be a real cow dog. He tracked the cow to the gully where she'd given birth to her calf. Then he held her back while Travis picked up the calf and carried it to the barn.

The next morning, a stranger on horseback rode up to the house. "Morning, Ma'am," he said to Katie. "I'm Burn Sanderson, from down near Santone. Bud Searcy told me you folks had an old stray dog that might be the one I lost."

Katie's heart sank, but she said to Arliss, "Go fetch Old Yeller."

When the two came back, Old Yeller pounced on Sanderson, barking happily. Arliss watched silently, then burst out, "He's my dog! You can't take my dog!"

"You really want that thievin' old cow dog?" Sanderson asked.

Arliss nodded wordlessly.

"Whatcha got in that pocket to swap?"

Arliss dug in his pocket and proudly produced a horned toad.

"Finest lookin' horned toad I ever saw," said Sanderson. "I'll swap the dog for that fine horned toad, boy!"

Arliss looked at his mother and grinned from ear to ear.

For the next few days, Arliss played endlessly with Old Yeller. But as time passed, Travis began to think of Old Yeller as his dog—not his little brother's.

It was Travis who always had Old Yeller by his side, Travis who fed him, and Travis whom Old Yeller snuggled up to at night.

One day Travis took Old Yeller hunting for wild hogs. Old Yeller drove the fierce hogs towards the tree where Travis was waiting to lasso the smallest animal for branding. The first hog was no problem, but the second pulled him from the branch—right into the angry pack. Yeller was hurt badly before he drove the hogs away.

Travis's leg was badly cut, but he was able to carry Old Yeller to a hiding place in a rock pile. "You got to stay here 'til I get help," he told the injured dog. "Otherwise, those hogs could come back and get you."

When Travis got home, Katie bandaged his leg while he told her what had happened. "We've got to go to Old Yeller *now*, Ma. Old Yeller is hurt real bad!"

"All right son," said Katie, gathering up her needle and thread.

Old Yeller licked Travis gratefully,
as Katie looked at the dog's wounds.
"Oh, Travis!" she said. "It's gonna take
a lot more than this thread to sew him
up. Quick—pull a few hairs from
Jumper's tail."

When Katie finished, they carried
Old Yeller home.

Lisbeth Searcy came to visit Travis the next day carrying a yellow puppy. "This here's one of Miss Prissy's puppies," she said. "Old Yeller is their pa."

"He's pretty!" said Arliss, patting the puppy. "Is he for me?"

"If Travis says so," Lisbeth answered.

Travis nodded and said, "I got me a dog already."

In the kitchen, Lisbeth's dad was telling Katie stories of wild-animal bites that carried the deadly disease called rabies. "It's all over the countryside," he said gloomily. "Hope that dog of yours don't get it from them hog bites. It turns the critters mad, and you have to shoot 'em."

"That's enough, Mr. Searcy!" said Katie sharply. Katie saw him to the door, then made up a bed for Lisbeth, who was staying for a few days.

That night, Travis heard his mother scream and ran outside with a rifle. "A wolf!" cried Katie, huddled by the fire. "Shoot it!"

Travis aimed, but he didn't dare fire—Old Yeller had attacked the wolf, which fought back savagely. At last, Travis had a clear shot, and the wolf dropped to the ground. Beside him, Old Yeller lay wounded.

Fighting tears, Katie said to Travis, "No wolf in his right mind would have come that close to the house, son. That wolf was mad, and Old Yeller's been bitten. He's got rabies now."

"We don't know for certain!" cried Travis. "We can't shoot Old Yeller! I'll lock him up 'till we see if he's sick."

Katie agreed, and they put Old Yeller in the corn crib. It could take a month for signs of the disease to appear.

For two weeks Old Yeller ate well and showed no bad effects from the wolf bites. Travis hoped that he could soon free his dog. But that night, he found Old Yeller lying down beside his dish. He growled at Travis, then bared his teeth in a snarl. Travis backed out of the corn crib, his heart hammering.

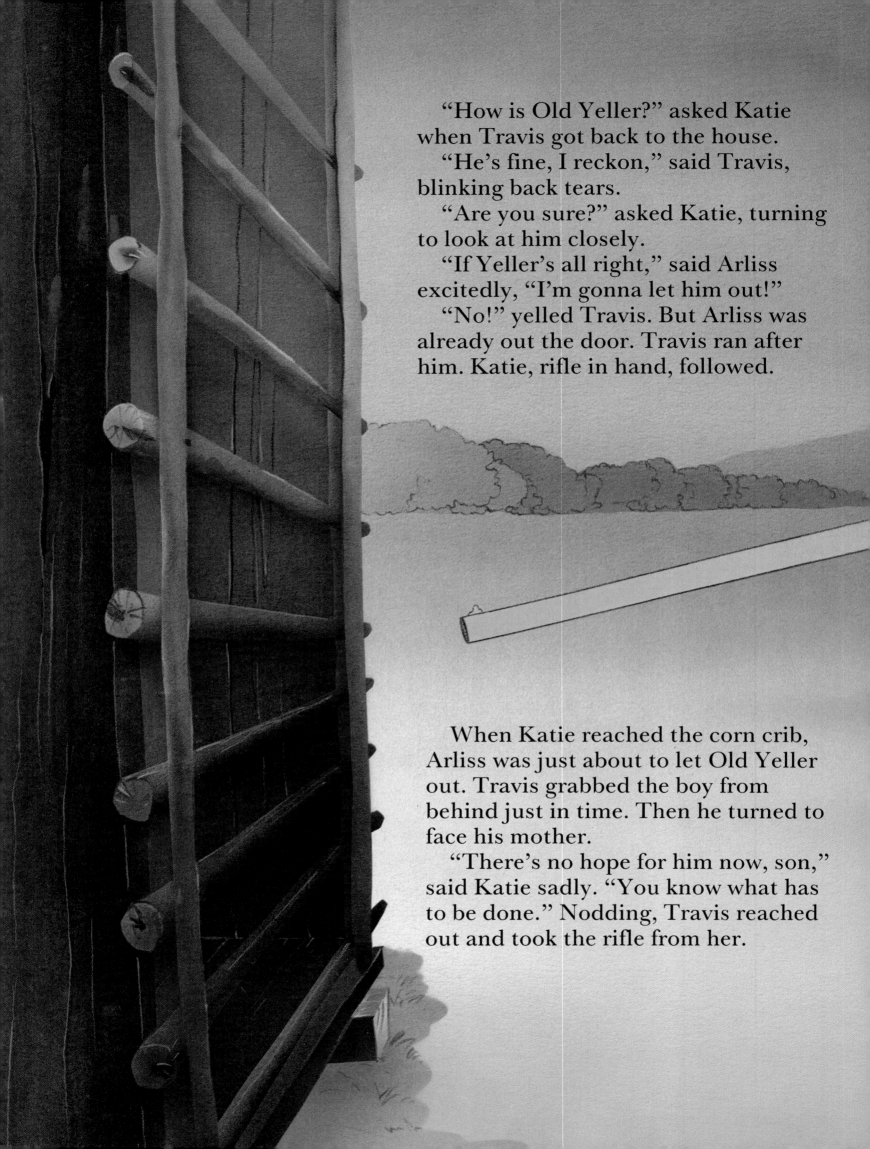

"How is Old Yeller?" asked Katie when Travis got back to the house.

"He's fine, I reckon," said Travis, blinking back tears.

"Are you sure?" asked Katie, turning to look at him closely.

"If Yeller's all right," said Arliss excitedly, "I'm gonna let him out!"

"No!" yelled Travis. But Arliss was already out the door. Travis ran after him. Katie, rifle in hand, followed.

When Katie reached the corn crib, Arliss was just about to let Old Yeller out. Travis grabbed the boy from behind just in time. Then he turned to face his mother.

"There's no hope for him now, son," said Katie sadly. "You know what has to be done." Nodding, Travis reached out and took the rifle from her.

The grief the family felt for Old
Yeller was lightened by Jim Coates's
return. "It's Papa!" cried Arliss, the
first to spot Jim riding into the yard.
   Jim hugged his wife and son and
showed them the wonderful presents
he'd brought from Kansas—a store-
bought dress for Katie, an Indian
headdress for Arliss, and for Travis, the
horse he'd always wanted.

While Katie told Jim about Old Yeller, Travis and Lisbeth were talking beside the corral. Arliss walked up and handed Lisbeth the puppy. Lisbeth took the pup and gave him to Travis. "I wish you could come to like him," she said. "He's part of Old Yeller."

Travis held the puppy as his parents came into the yard. It was good to have his dad home again.

"Your mama told me about your dog, son," said Jim. "I'm mighty proud of how you faced up to the problem head-on. Life sure can be hurtful sometimes."

"Yessir," said Travis, putting down the puppy, which started chewing at his boot.

"But the good times help keep you going," added Jim, as Young Yeller took off across the grass.

Travis nodded. "Reckon it's time I started teachin' that pup to earn his keep," he said. Then he and his father went into the cabin together.